Little Bear
and the Big Fight

Jutta Langreuter and Vera Sobat

The Millbrook Press
Brookfield, Connecticut

It should have been a very happy day at Bear Kindergarten. The cubs were working with brand-new blocks of clay, and they could make whatever they wanted.

Little Bear used the clay to make farm animals. His best friend, Brandon, made what he always made with clay—pink flamingos!

"Who has the pink clay?" asked Little Bear.

"I do," answered Brandon.

"I need some of it," said Little Bear. "I'm going to make a fat pig for my farm."

"Use another color," said Brandon. "I'm making a whole lake full of flamingos, and I need all the pink."

"I *can't* use another color," answered Little Bear. "Pigs have to be pink and you're supposed to share!"

"Too bad!" shouted Brandon as he gathered up all the pink clay. "I got the pink first. Make your silly old pig yellow."

This made Little Bear angry. "Give it to me, Brandon, and give it to me now!" he shouted, reaching for the pink clay.

Still clutching the clay, Brandon wriggled away from Little Bear and raced around the table and into the bathroom.

Now Little Bear was *very* angry. He swept Brandon's flamingos off the table and onto the floor. Then he stomped on them.

"That wasn't nice, Little Bear," said Danny, picking up the clay car he had made and taking it to a safer place.

Little Bear didn't care if the other cubs thought he was nice. He stood in the middle of the room and glared at them. "I can be even meaner than that," he said.

Everyone heard the sound of a toilet flushing. Brandon came out of the bathroom and looked at Little Bear. "I decided I'd rather flush away the pink clay than share it with you," Brandon announced proudly.

"Oh, yeah?" said Little Bear. "Well, look what I did to your flamingos, Bratty Brandon!"

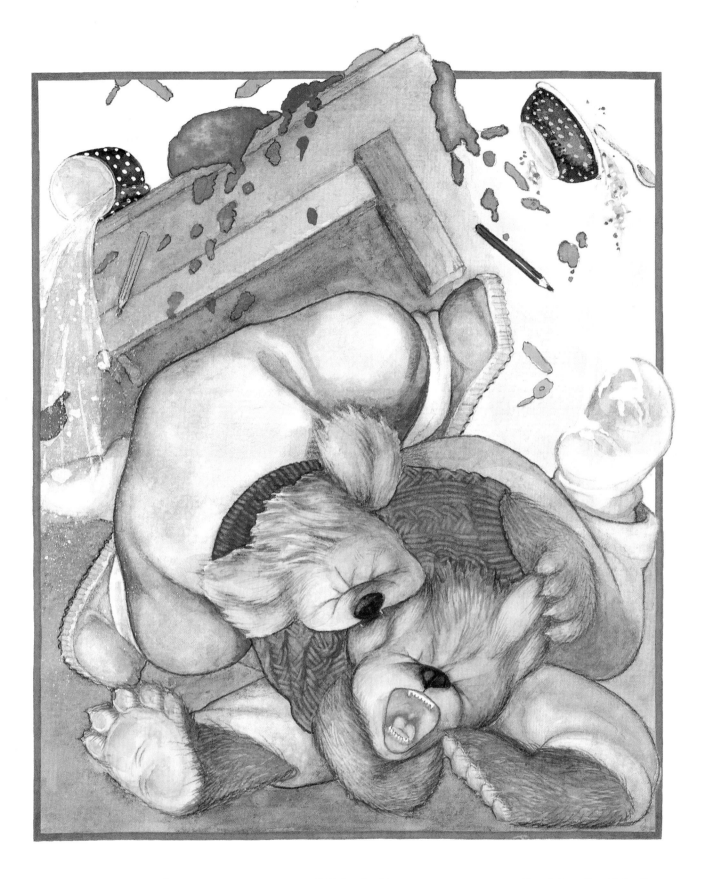

Now Brandon was angry and Little Bear was angry. Suddenly, Little Bear jumped on Brandon and bit his ear!

Ms. Brown, the kindergarten teacher, rushed over and used all her strength to separate the two cubs.

"Stop right now, Little Bear," she said as she pulled him away from Brandon.

"Owww!" cried Brandon. "Little Bear bit me!"

"What were you thinking of?" the teacher asked Little Bear. "Why would you ever bite your friend Brandon?"

Brandon's ear began to bleed. Ms. Brown went to get a bandage. Danny checked the toilet to see if the clay had clogged it. It hadn't.

"It wasn't my fault," said Little Bear. "He wouldn't share."

"No matter what happens, Little Bear, friends shouldn't bite," said Ms. Brown, bandaging Brandon's ear and patting him. "Or fight," she said to Brandon.

The other bear cubs all nodded and looked away from Little Bear.

"I didn't mean to do it so hard," said Little Bear. He spoke so quietly that no one heard him.

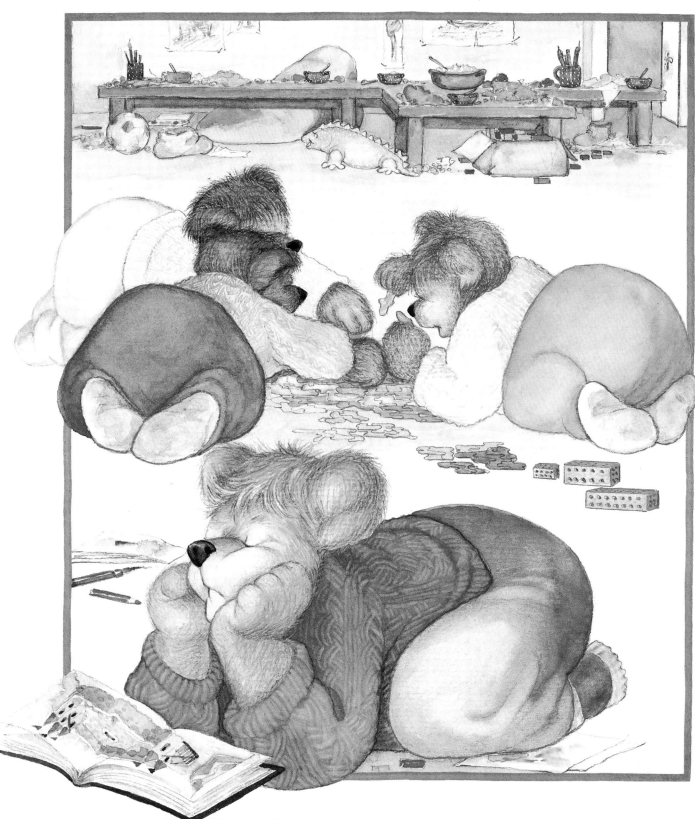

Later, when all the other cubs worked together on a jigsaw puzzle, Little Bear didn't join in. He looked at a picture book, but he really didn't see very much. He felt as if he were all alone.

On the way home Mama said, "Ms. Brown told me you hurt
Brandon today, Little Bear. Isn't he your best friend?"
"Not anymore," said Little Bear. "He started it. He wouldn't share."

When Little Bear arrived at school the next morning, he thought about telling Brandon he was sorry, but then he thought about the pink clay and how selfish Brandon was, and he felt angry.

None of the cubs paid any attention to Little Bear. They let Brandon, with his big new bandage, be King of the Castle. And Little Bear got mad all over again.

Even at bedtime, when Papa came to say good night, Little Bear was still angry . . .

. . . and the angry feeling lasted all through the next day. It didn't feel good.

That night Mama said to Papa, "Look, dear, here's a picture of Little Bear on the first day of school. That was the day he met Brandon, remember?

"I do," said Papa. "Brandon and Little Bear were as happy as two cubs in a cave. Good friends are hard to find."

Little Bear remembered. He remembered the happy feeling of
having Brandon for his friend. But now it was easier to stay angry.

Mama had some clay for Little Bear to bring to school the next day. "I thought you might want to share this clay with Brandon," she said to Little Bear.

"No," said Little Bear. "He's not my friend anymore."

"Be careful of what you say, Little Bear," warned Papa. "It might come true."

At recess Little Bear still didn't feel like playing with the other cubs, so he walked over to a corner of the playground. All of a sudden, Brandon came over to him. "If I say I'm sorry, will you say so too, Little Bear?" asked Brandon.

Little Bear thought about saying yes. Even though he knew the fight was all Brandon's fault, he really missed being with him. But Little Bear took so long to answer that Brandon turned and walked away. Little Bear felt worse than ever.

All through snack Little Bear thought about Brandon. He truly did feel sorry that he bit him. Who cared if Brandon had started the fight?

Would saying "I'm sorry" make all the bad feelings go away?

Later that day, the class took turns on the merry-go-round. Little Bear was in line ahead of Brandon, but when Little Bear's turn came, he said, "You go first, Brandon. I'm really sorry that I bit you."

"And I'm sorry that I didn't share," said Brandon. "Really sorry."

"Friends again?" he asked.
"Best friends!" said Little Bear.

Little Bear was happy to be Brandon's friend again. To celebrate, the next day he brought Brandon's favorite snack to school.

"Your special banana, Mr. Best Friend!" he said with a bow.

Later, the class made kites. "Will you hold this string tight for me?" Brandon asked Little Bear. When the string pinched Little Bear's finger, Brandon said, "I'm sorry, Little Bear. I'm *very* sorry."

When Little Bear accidentally pulled the string off Brandon's kite, he quickly said, "Ooops! I'm sorry, Brandon. I'm *very* sorry." The cubs looked at each other and laughed.

"I'll race you to the field, Brandon!" yelled Little Bear. It really didn't matter who was right and who was wrong, it just felt great to have his best friend back again.

First published in the United States of America in 1998 by
The Millbrook Press, Inc.
2 Old New Milford Road, Brookfield, CT 06804

English language text copyright © 1998 by The Millbrook Press

Copyright © 1997 arsEdition, Friedrichstrasse 9,
80801 Munich, Germany

Library of Congress Cataloging-in-Publication Data
on file at the Library of Congress

ISBN 0-7613-0403-7 (lib. bdg.) ISBN 0-7613-0375-8 (pbk.)

Printed in Belgium